Fisherman FRED

Written by Tony D. Triggs

With an original ending by Michael Twinn

Illustrated by Toni Goffe

Child's Play (International) Ltd

Swindon   Toronto   Sydney   New York

© M. Twinn 1994   ISBN 0-85953-932-6   Printed in Singapore

A catalogue reference for this book is available
from the British Library

Fisherman Fred went fishing each night...

And, every day, he rode around the town
on his rusty old bike, calling,
"Fish for sale! Fish for sale!"

He had almost no time left for anything else.

One day, Fred was selling fish
to his friend, Bill, when he had an idea.

"I'll give up my bike and sell fish from my front room!
You are a genius with paint, Bill.
Why don't you paint a sign to go over my front door?"

Bill came at once. Soon the sign was gleaming across the front of Fred's house.

But very few customers came to buy fish.

Later that day, a man pointed at the sign and laughed.

"You don't need to say the fish is fresh.
You couldn't sell it, otherwise!"

"Perhaps, he's right," thought Fisherman Fred,
when the man had gone.
"I'd better hide the word **fresh**".

Fred climbed his ladder and nailed a board over part of the sign.

Now, there were only three words, not four. But very few customers came to buy fish.

A girl came along with her dog.

"Why does your sign say **here**?
The sign is here, so the fish must be here, too, mustn't it?"

So, Fred decided to hide the word **here**.

Now, there were only two words on the sign.
But very few customers came to buy fish.

Next, a woman stared at the sign.

"Surely, you don't need to say **sold**," she giggled.
"We know, you don't give your fish away!"

Fred agreed.
He nailed on another board.

Only a single word was left.
But very few customers came to buy fish.

Then, Charlie Bloggs, the policeman, said,

"You don't need a sign, at all.
Why say **fish**, when you've sold fish for years?"

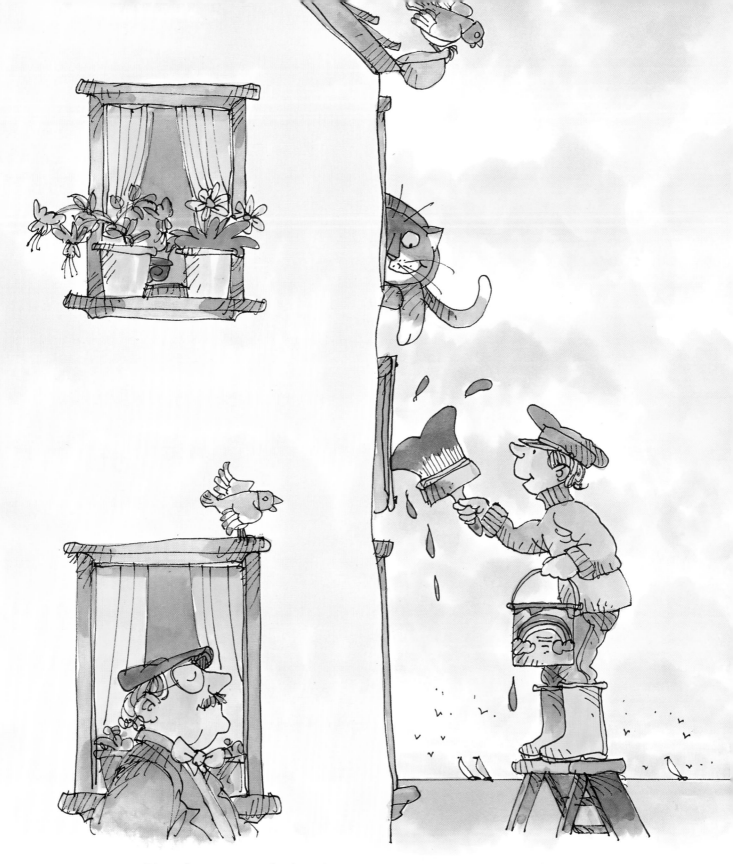

Fred covered the last word.
Then, he fetched some brown paint
and made the boards look like new.

But very few customers came to the house.

Just as he finished, an old man came up.
He wanted to buy a can of paint.

"I can tell by the smell that you sell paint," he said.
"But wouldn't it be better to have a proper sign?"

"Aha!" sighed Fred. "So, I do need a sign, after all!"

He climbed his ladder and took off
one of the painted boards.

But very few customers came to the house.

A boy whizzed by on his skateboard.
"Hello, Mr Fish!" he called rudely.

So, Fred took off another board.

Now, there were two words on the sign again.
But very few customers came to the house.

"They still think I sell my fish in the street," thought Fred.
"But I sell it here and the sign should say so."

Fred took off another board.

Now, there were three words again.
But very few customers came to the house.

Then, along came Bill.

"You've spoiled my sign," he said angrily.
"That big space in front of **fish** looks all wrong."

So, Fred took off the last board.

Now, there were four words on the sign again.
But, still, very few customers came to Fred's house.

In the meantime,
the fish wasn't so fresh.

Fred called the cats' home...
The lady was one
of his best customers.

"I'm afraid this fish is not fresh," explained Fred, "but it is FREE."

"Thank you," she said. "I'll come over right away.
I wondered what had happened to you."

Fred told her about the sign Bill had made.

"I noticed it at once," she smiled. "It is a lovely sign. But there is one thing wrong with it...

"Now, you go fishing and I will talk to Bill."

It was still dark, when Fred arrived home.

The next morning, when he drew back the curtains,
all his old customers were waiting outside.

Fred rubbed his eyes.
He hurried to wash and get dressed.

When he opened the door, everyone cheered.

The lady from the cats' home was there.
The cats had come, too, to say thank you to Fred.

"You forgot to put your name on the sign," she said.
"**Fred** stands for honesty and cheerfulness and fresh fish."

"Nothing
is more important
than your good name!"

Other titles illustrated
or written and illustrated by Toni Goffe:

The Giant that sneezed
The Prince who wrote a letter
Ma, you're driving me crazy!
The Monster
How to be rich
Relax
Chief – Who is in Charge?
No Smoking
President Citizen
Bully for You
War and Peace
Charm School